On the Trail of OLD TOM

Michael Wagner
Illustrated by Leigh Hobbs

Contents

THOMSON
™
NELSON

stralia · Canada · Mexico · Singapore · Spain · United Kingdom · United States

Old Tom – My Hero!

Ahh, Old Tom – my hero.
The mischievous, messy,
one-eyed international
superstar of books and
television. He's given
me a goal in life.
I want to be just
like him.

Leigh HOBBS.

He does what he wants, and he
gets away with anything. What a life!
But how does he do it?
If only I could talk to him. Problem is, he doesn't speak.

The only way I'm going to find out what Old Tom is really like is by talking to the people around him.

I'll talk to his creator, Leigh Hobbs, some of the people involved in his books and television series, and a few of the other characters in his world. Then I'll know just what makes him tick!

Let's start at the beginning. How was he created?

Chapter 2

From First Drawings to International Superstar

Old Tom wasn't always an orange, one-eyed international superstar. In the beginning he wasn't really anything at all – just a collection of ideas floating around Leigh Hobbs' head. Ideas like:

- a cat who behaves like a seven-year-old boy
- a character who always does what he wants
- a character with the name Old Tom.

Gradually, these ideas came together to form one creature. It wasn't quite Old Tom, but it was getting close.

Old Tom changed over time. Here's how he looked a short time after the first drawing.

Old Tom's personality revealed itself, bit by bit, over time. As it did, he became less **obnoxious** and more funny. Basically, he cleaned up his act.

Now, he looks like this ...

Leigh HOBBS

When this final version of Old Tom emerged, Leigh felt his naughty little tomcat was ready for the world. Not too nasty and not too cute, Old Tom was just right.

A publisher Leigh had been working with was also impressed. She asked Leigh to write and illustrate a book about Old Tom. Leigh was delighted.

Unfortunately, when it was done, the publisher wasn't so sure any more. She had lost confidence in several things about the book, including the way Old Tom looked. She wasn't certain, for example, that he should have a bung eye.

Leigh believed he'd got Old Tom right and he wasn't keen to change him. Unable to agree, Leigh and the publisher parted company, leaving Old Tom without a home.

Even though Old Tom had no one to publish him, Leigh believed he could find him a new home. He sent the book to other publishers. It was rejected four or five times before an editor at Penguin Books saw it, and loved it.

Author Note

Lots of famous books have been rejected by publishers. Some are rejected many times before becoming best sellers. I've also had my stories rejected. So, how does it feel to work on something for months, finally get it right, then be rejected? Frustrating! Embarrassing! Frightening! But, when you do get your work published, you forget all that, because it feels fantastic!

Old Tom's editor at Penguin was Erica Wagner. The moment Erica saw a picture of the orange tomcat slumped in a chair with his feet up, she wanted to work with him.

At the time, I was the parent of a seven-year-old boy who could sometimes be a little bit wild, but was also extremely lovable. That's why I fell in love with Old Tom. He's like a lot of boys I know. He's naughty, but nice and you never know what he's going to do next.

Erica Wagner

A few years after the first Old Tom books were published, the unpredictable **feline** became the star of his own television series – simply called *Old Tom*.

One of the people who helped put him onto the small screen was Tim Brooke-Hunt, who was a director with the Australian **animation** studio Yoram Gross.

Tim knew Leigh and respected him as an artist. He also knew the books and was certain Old Tom would look great on television.

We saw the Old Tom books as the classics of tomorrow. I felt the books cried out for animation. And I felt the image of Old Tom would translate well to the screen. He was distinctive and fresh in a way we knew would appeal to both television people and children. Basically, he had a 'stand-out' look.

Tim Brooke-Hunt

Leigh HOBBS

Getting Old Tom onto television was sometimes difficult for Leigh. For the first time he had to let other artists draw and animate his cherished characters.

While it was hard to give up control over the drawing of Old Tom images, in the end Leigh felt Yoram Gross did a good job with the look of Old Tom and his world.

And when Leigh first saw Old Tom move, in a tiny piece of animation, he said it was like watching his first child learn to walk.

Chapter 3

Creating a Superstar

In an Old Tom story, Leigh creates a funny, warm world from nothing but paper, pencils, paint and his imagination.

Some authors begin the process of creating a story with a funny situation or the first part of a long story, but Leigh starts with a character.

> None of the characters I come up with are based on only one person. They're all a mixture of people I've met and a little bit of me as well. Most importantly, they have to have a real personality.
>
> *Leigh Hobbs*

Horrible Harriet is another of Leigh's unusual characters.

Unusual, naughty, lovable characters interest Leigh most, and when he's found one he likes, he starts imagining it in drawings. But rather than dream up funny drawings himself, Leigh waits for ideas to come to him.

Old Tom Goes To Mars began with the idea of **portholes**. Leigh likes portholes. He wanted to see Old Tom peering through one. He decided the porthole Old Tom looks through should be attached to a rocket.

When he'd drawn Old Tom looking through the porthole of a rocket, he thought of a sentence that seemed to fit: 'At 9.15 exactly Old Tom left Earth for Mars.'

Leigh sent the drawing and the line of text to Erica, his editor at Penguin Books, who agreed it was a great start to the next book. Several months later, *Old Tom Goes To Mars* was launched.

Interestingly, neither the porthole drawing nor the line of text ended up in the book – but the ideas behind them certainly did.

Old Tom – Man Of Mystery was also inspired by a single idea for a drawing. Actually, it started with a drawing from an earlier Old Tom book.

There's a picture in *Old Tom's Guide To Being Good* of Old Tom standing on top of his owner Angela Throgmorton's fridge wearing a mask and cape. When Leigh looked back at that picture long after it was published, he thought Old Tom looked like a 'man of mystery'.

Slowly, the single idea of Old Tom being a 'man of mystery' became an entire book.

Author Note

Writers rely on having lots of ideas. To make sure I never forget any, I keep them in a journal. Some ideas seem crazy, but I write them down anyway. My journal includes notes like 'using a sheep as a lawn mower' and 'the guinea pig race', which may seem odd now, but might one day inspire a brilliant story! Well, you never know ...

Once the first drawing for a book is done, the book has a direction. Other ideas for drawings come bit by bit. Some of the first ideas might appear at the end of the book, and some of the last ideas at the beginning.

Gradually, these unrelated ideas fit together into one complete story.

That's how the Old Tom books are born.

Author Note

Not all authors work this way: some, like Leigh, start without knowing how the story is going to end, but others won't start until they know just what's going to happen. I prefer to know the ending before I start writing. Otherwise I feel nervous that I may not be able to come up with a good finish.

Chapter 4

The Fun (and Not So Fun) Life of an Illustrator

Because drawing is fun, we tend to think of the life of an artist as pretty relaxed. And, of course, it is enjoyable, but professional illustrators also have to display discipline and patience.

Some drawings come to Leigh all at once, so that he can finish them very quickly. Others take days to complete. Leigh once spent three days on a painting, only to throw it out and start again. That part of an illustrator's life is not much fun.

While these difficult drawings can be terribly frustrating, Leigh believes they can also be of great benefit. In struggling with an illustration day after day, until it's just right, Leigh often learns something new about his art and himself.

This, he believes, forces him to become a better artist.

And while his drawings may look like they've been quickly thrown together, they are the product of a great deal of experience and effort.

> Sometimes the drawings that appear the simplest have taken the longest time to do.
>
> *Leigh Hobbs*

The life of an artist is not all fun, but in the end there is nothing Leigh would rather do.

> As difficult as drawing can be sometimes, it can also be extremely rewarding and enjoyable!
>
> *Leigh Hobbs*

Leigh in his studio.

Chapter 5

Is Old Tom Just Like Leigh?

While authors write about lots of characters in all sorts of situations, many authors are really writing about themselves. It makes sense when you think about it – the one person in the world you really understand is you, and if you want to write a book that feels very real, write it about yourself.

The characters you write about may not look like you, may not be the same gender as you, may not even be human, and they may end up in situations you'll never encounter, but they can still be based on you.

Author Note

It's not a bad thing when authors write mostly about themselves. Although they use the same basic character time and again, they are able to use their own experiences to produce fresh adventures and stories for their characters to participate in. I once heard someone say that writers are like farmers, tilling th same earth year after year, but always producing fresh harvests.

Therefore, is Old Tom really like Leigh Hobbs?

I think I am Old Tom in a way. There's a lot of my childhood in the books, even details like certain furniture in Angela's house and the clothesline in her backyard.

Leigh Hobbs

Old Tom is noisy, messy, lazy and mischievous. Leigh is not.

As a boy, Leigh was at times shy – in fact, he didn't like to draw attention to himself. He was a hard worker and quite tidy. So, Leigh's not like Old Tom at all, right?

Not exactly. Leigh was just like Old Tom in one way –
in his thoughts. He might not have behaved like Old Tom,
but deep down, he wanted to. Rather than draw attention
to himself, Leigh would just draw, and his characters would
draw attention to themselves.

Oh, and Leigh and Old Tom also like the same sorts of
food. But while Leigh might enjoy eating a piece of cake,
Old Tom likes to have an entire cake!

So, yes, Old Tom is a lot like Leigh.

Old Tom's table manners have left Angela embarrassed often.

Chapter 6

Leigh, the Artist

As we've found out, when Leigh dreams up characters for his books, he imagines going back to his childhood. So what was his childhood like?

When Leigh Was a Boy

Leigh spent most of his childhood in a country town. His father was a schoolteacher, his mother a dressmaker, and he has a sister who's three years younger than him.

Leigh, on his bike, with his mother and sister.

Author Note

Leigh asked me not to include the names of any of his family. They prefer not to be known, otherwise they might lose some of their privacy. I feel the same way about my privacy. I wonder if Old Tom does too?

Leigh remembers his childhood as being safe and secure and that he always wanted to be an artist. He drew from as early as he can remember.

In 1957, when Leigh was four, his father gave him a drawing board. He still uses it today.

Leigh's drawing board.

At Leigh's request, his father gave him an alarm clock. Leigh wanted to get up at six o'clock every morning so that he had time to draw before heading off to school. Leigh still gets up very early and starts his working day before eight o'clock.

When Leigh was about five he loved drawing castles, pirates and pirate ships. When he was a little older, he liked drawing battles with knights in armour.

The Emerging Artist

At first Leigh drew because he loved it. But as he got older, he became more **critical**. He wanted to draw like his favourite artists.

He loved the work of English artist Ronald Searle and was fascinated by the way an artist could create an entire world, with its own atmosphere and mood. He also loved the fact that this world could make people laugh.

Author Note
I really like a saying I once heard on the radio: "I don't want to be the best, I want to be my best." I think that's a great way to live.

I've always tried to do my best work. That means experimenting with ink, paints and brushes, inventing different ways to do things.

Leigh Hobbs

Leigh's Artistic Adulthood

After graduating from art school, Leigh worked at Sydney's Luna Park restoring the carousel and creating two characters called 'Larry and Lizzy Luna'. The sculptures are now housed in Sydney's Powerhouse Museum.

Leigh also taught art in secondary schools for years while continuing to practise as an artist. His artworks are held in private art collections, and in galleries in cities and in country towns.

In 1999, Leigh designed the colour scheme for the entrance to Melbourne's Luna Park.

Leigh designed and made this teapot to look like Flinders Street Station in Melbourne. It is in the National Gallery of Victoria.

This is one of Leigh's earliest paintings: can you see a house that looks very much like Angela's house and a cat that looks a little like Old Tom?

From a little boy who loved to draw, Leigh became what he'd always wanted to be – an artist. And his best-known creation is Old Tom!

Chapter 7

Angela Throgmorton: the Interview

Finding out about Leigh is helpful for understanding Old Tom, but what about the person who has cared for Old Tom for most of his life? Angela Throgmorton has raised Old Tom since he was left, as a baby, in a basket on her doorstep.

I spoke with Angela about her life with Old Tom.

Michael: *What did you think of Old Tom when you first saw him wrapped in a bundle on your doorstep?*

Angela: I thought, oh there's a gorgeous baby.

Michael: *Was he a difficult youngster?*

Angela: He was naughty, and a bit lazy at times, but he was always my baby.

Michael: *Is he fun to have around?*

Angela: Yes, though I have to keep my eye on him because he very easily gets out of hand. Sometimes he doesn't know when to stop.

Michael: *Do you think other people really understand Old Tom?*

Angela: Some people do – children do. Some people are frightened of him, especially the neighbours. They think he looks like a monster, but he's good most of the time. I've asked them to babysit at times, but suddenly they'll be going on overseas trips, or something ...

Leigh HOBBS

Michael: *Old Tom can be unpredictable at times; how was he when you visited the Queen?*

Angela: He was on his best behaviour and for some reason the Queen really liked him. They got on very well. She showed us around the palace, and I remember she pointed out the throne to Old Tom. I suspect Old Tom may have sat on it when we weren't watching.

Michael: *Do you mind the way Old Tom keeps his room?*

Angela: I must say I do. I like a tidy home and I would prefer that there weren't chicken bones left in his bed. He drags all sorts of things in from the street. I never know what I'm going to find.

Michael: *What are your hopes and dreams for Old Tom?*

Angela: I hope that he will, at some stage in the future, tidy his room. I would also like him to help around the home a little bit more.

Michael: *Some people would wonder why you put up with Old Tom's mess and antics – why do you?*

Angela: He's family. He's my baby. He's grown up a little bit and put on quite a bit of weight, but despite all his faults and his untidiness, just between you and me, I adore him.

Michael: *What do you think of Leigh Hobbs?*

Angela: He's a bit of a mystery to me. Hmmm ...

Chapter 8

Old Tom's Friends and Foes: the Vox Pop

Now we know how Leigh and Angela see Old Tom, but what about the other people around him?
I asked some of the characters in Old Tom's world what they think of him.

Vox Pop: What do you think of Old Tom?

Lavinia
(Angela's best friend):
It's disgusting! A monster!

Author Note

A vox pop is a series of interviews with different people, where you ask them all the same question. The words 'vox pop' come from the Latin *vox populi*, which means 'voice of the people'. Vox pops are don quite often on television and radio. I used to work in radio and did them every now and then. It's a great way of seeing how different people feel about the same topic.

The postman: Sometimes he's in the letterbox. Sometimes he's behind the bird bath. You never know where he's going to pop up. I think he sets out to upset me.

Percy the pirate: The little fellow would make a champion pirate. He's good company, friendly and very funny. He also looks the part in a pirate hat, and boy can he dance!

The Queen of England: Old Tom is simply charming and rather sweet in his own special way. He's welcome at the palace any time – as long as we have a little advance warning. That way we can put away any royal breakables and perhaps check that the royal vacuum cleaner is working properly.

Chapter 9

The Real Old Tom

Okay, I think I know Old Tom better now. I've met the important people close to him: Leigh and, of course, his special friend Angela. This is how I'd sum up the real Old Tom:

1 Old Tom likes to relax ... often.

2 Old Tom is not frightened of anything ... except housework.

3 Old Tom thinks he's pretty handsome.

4 Old Tom has a sweet tooth, especially for cakes, chocolates and ice cream.

5 As well as cakes, Old Tom loves ... Angela.

Glossary

animation   the filming of drawings to create the appearance of movement

critical   making judgements about something

feline   another word for cat

obnoxious   rude and unpleasant

portholes   small, round windows found in ships and other means of transport, including spacecraft

Further Reading

Read all about Old Tom, and Horrible Harriet, in the following titles by Leigh Hobbs.

Old Tom, Penguin Books Australia Ltd, 1994

Old Tom at the Beach, Penguin Books Australia Ltd, 1995

Old Tom Goes to Mars, Penguin Books Australia Ltd, 1997

Old Tom's Guide to Being Good, Penguin Books Australia Ltd, 1998

Old Tom's Holiday, ABC Books, 2002

Old Tom Man of Mystery, ABC Books, 2003

Horrible Harriet, Allen & Unwin, 2001

Website

www.leighhobbs.com

See more on Leigh Hobbs, his books and artworks, and of course Old Tom!